Can I Pray with My Eyes Open?

Susan Taylor Brown & *Illustrated by* Garin Baker

HYPERION BOOKS FOR CHILDREN & *New York*

Printed in Hong Kong.

FIRST EDITION

1 3 5 7 9 10 8 6 4 2

This book is set in 24/30-point Calisto.
The art for this book was executed in oil paint.

℘

Library of Congress Cataloging-in-Publication Data

Brown, Susan (Susan Taylor).
Can I pray with my eyes open?/Susan Brown; illustrated by Gavin Baker—1st. ed.
p. cm.
Summary: In rhyming text, a child wonders how and when and where is the perfect way
to say a prayer and realizes that there is no wrong time or place for prayer.
ISBN 0-7868-0328-2 (trade)—ISBN 0-7868-2273-2 (lib. ed.)
1. Prayer—Juvenile literature. [1. Prayer.] I. Baker, Gavin, ill. II. Title.
BL560.B66 1999
291.4'3-dc21   98-51676

FOR MY MOTHER, DARLENE TENNELL,

who never stops giving me second chances. Thanks, mom.

—S. T. B.

&

THE WORK DONE IN THIS BOOK IS DEDICATED TO MY FAMILY—

Jerilyn, Amanda, and Harrison—who patiently posed and inspired me.

Can I Pray With My Eyes Open? gave me an opportunity to preserve,

with paintings, a fleeting moment in our children's young lives,

when excitement, joy, and questions go hand in hand.

—G. B.

I wondered how and when and where
was the perfect way to say a prayer.

Must every prayer
be one that's spoken?
And can I pray
with my eyes open?

When I go swimming in the creek,
or play a game of hide-and-seek,

Or even when I climb a tree,
if I'm outside, can You hear me?

When I'm under the covers, out of sight,
or listening to music or flying a kite,

When I don't know
what I should do,
is that a time
to talk to You?

When I Rollerblade or ride my bike,
can I pray any time I like?

If I cross my fingers or stand on my head,
or get mad and my face turns red,

If I'm skipping rope or playing ball,
or walking backward down the hall,

When building castles at the beach,
will You still be within my reach?

When I look up and count the stars,
or climb upon the monkey bars,

When I'm in a car, a boat, or train,
does every prayer have to be the same?

I thought it over
through and through.
Then I shared
my thoughts with You.

I got an answer right away. . . .
There's no wrong time or place to pray.